NEW EDITION

Wide Range Readers

GREEN BOOK 3

Fred J. Schonell
Phyllis Flowerdew

Oliver & Boyd

Acknowledgments

We are grateful to the following for supplying photographs and giving permission for their use: Lynn Abercrombie, pp. 88–89; British Travel Authority, p. 103.

The photographs on pp. 100 and 101 are reproduced by Gracious Permission of Her Majesty the Queen.

Illustrated by Moira Chesmur, Carol Holmes, Harry Horse, Peter Joyce, Tony Morris and David Simon.

Oliver & Boyd
Longman House
Burnt Mill
Harlow
Essex CM20 2JE
An Imprint of Longman Group UK Ltd

First published 1951
Second edition 1965
Third edition 1976
Fourth edition 1985
Sixth impression 1992

ISBN 0 05 003751 X

Set in 14/20pt Monophoto Plantin
Produced by Longman Group (FE) Ltd
Print in Hong Kong

The publisher's policy is to use paper manufactured from sustainable forests.

Preface

The Wide Range Readers are planned to provide graded reading practice for junior school children. Because children of 7–11 have a wide range of reading needs and attainments, there are three parallel series—Blue, Green and Red books—to provide plenty of material to suit the interests and reading ages of every child.

Books 1–4 are graded by half yearly reading ages, for use by appropriate groups within a class. Book 1 should provide an easy read for children with a reading age of about 7–7$\frac{1}{2}$. Children with reading ages below 7 are recommended to use the Wide Range Starters.

The controlled vocabulary of the series makes the books suitable for the following reading ages:

6$\frac{1}{2}$–7	**Starter Books**—Blue, Green and Red
7–7$\frac{1}{2}$	**Book 1**—Blue, Green and Red
7$\frac{1}{2}$–8	**Book 2**—Blue, Green and Red
8–8$\frac{1}{2}$	**Book 3**—Blue, Green and Red
8$\frac{1}{2}$–9	**Book 4**—Blue, Green and Red
9+	**Book 5**—Blue, Green and Red
10+	**Book 6**—Blue, Green and Red
11+	**Book 7**—Red only
12+	**Book 8**—Red only

Where to Find the Stories

Pirello the Dancing Horse

Bright lights. Cheerful music. The soft
sawdust of the circus ring. That was the
life Pirello loved. That was the only life for
him. He had been a circus horse for as long
as he could remember. He had been taught
and looked after, and loved by Carlo, his
master. He would do anything in the world
for Carlo.

So tonight was just like other nights, with Carlo giving orders in a gentle voice and Pirello dancing for him.

Pirello danced on four legs—one, two, three, hop—one, two, three, hop. Pirello danced on two legs, with his front legs in the air—one, two, three, hop—one, two, three, hop. Pirello bowed, and Carlo bowed, and the people clapped and cheered.

So it was just like any other night. Bright lights. Cheerful music. The soft sawdust of the circus ring. Yet Pirello the dancing horse knew that it wasn't like other nights. Something was different. Something was wrong, and as soon as his act was over, Carlo told him what it was.

He took Pirello to his sleeping-box, and he pressed his face against Pirello's silky, grey head, and he said,

"We've had the last dance, Pirello. We've had the last dance." Pirello was puzzled. What did his master mean?

"We have to say goodbye," added Carlo
sadly. "It's a small circus. It has
never made much money. Mr Garry
is giving it up. Tomorrow he's selling
everything—the tents, the caravans, the
animals—even you."

Pirello gave a soft little cry. He
understood.

"If you really belonged to me, I would
take you away. If I had money to pay for
you, we'd never be parted. But I'm poor.
I must find another circus, and you must go
to the market to be sold."

Carlo said no more.   He only stood gazing at Pirello—his horse, his partner, his only friend.

Then he closed the door of the sleeping-box, and ran away into the night; and Pirello the dancing horse understood.

Next day he was sent to the winter market to be sold.   He stood silently, as one man after another came to look at him.   He didn't care who bought him.   He wanted Carlo and the circus life.   His heart was filled with sadness.

He was sold at last to a farmer.

"You're a fine, strong horse," said the
farmer. "You'll be able to pull the plough
for me."

So he took Pirello to a green field, beside
an old white farmhouse, and there he left him
for some time.

Then one morning, he led him out of the field, fixed him to a plough and took him to a great stretch of rough, brown earth.

"Gee up," said the farmer. Pirello pulled, and the plough moved behind him, digging up the brown earth in long, straight furrows. Pirello walked down the field to the end. Then he turned and went up the field.

Down the field and up the field he went, down and up, down and up. The earth lay in rich, brown furrows behind him, and a crowd of hungry birds followed him.

"You're a good horse," said the farmer. "You're a fine horse."

Pirello went on up and down the field, but his heart was sad. He saw trees stretching up to the blue sky. He saw grass swaying in the breeze.

Everything was beautiful but it wasn't part of the life he knew. He sighed for bright lights, cheerful music, and the soft sawdust

of a circus ring.   He sighed for Carlo his
master.

Suddenly in the middle of the field Pirello
began to dance.   He danced on four legs—
one, two, three, hop—one, two, three, hop.
The plough jerked and swayed, and the
furrows went criss-cross all over the field.
He danced on two legs, with his front legs in
the air.

"Stop!" cried the farmer. "Stop!"

But Pirello didn't stop. He was a dancing horse. He danced and danced until his act was done. Then he bowed to the trees and the blue sky. He bowed to the grass and the birds. Then he stood still.

When the spring market came, Pirello was taken to the town to be sold. His life as a farm horse had ended.

He stood silently in the market, as one man after another came to look at him. He didn't care who bought him. He wanted Carlo and the circus life.

He was sold at last to a man from a distant village.

"You're a fine, strong horse," said the man. "You'll be useful to me." So he rode Pirello down the roads and lanes, until he reached his home. Then he put him in a stable yard at the back of a shop, and left him there for some time.

Then one morning he led him out of the

yard, and fixed him to a cart, loaded with bottles of milk.

"Gee up!" said the milkman.

Pirello pulled and the milk cart moved behind him. Down the street he went, stopping when he was told and waiting while the milkman left milk at the houses.

Down the street went Pirello, then up the next and down the next—up and down, up and down, up and down.

"You're a good horse," said the milkman. "You're a fine horse."

Pirello went on up the streets and down the streets but his heart was sad. He saw red brick houses and little gardens. He saw cars and bicycles, and people and children. Everything was interesting but it wasn't part of the life he knew.

He sighed for bright lights, cheerful music, and the soft sawdust of a circus ring. He sighed for Carlo his master.

Suddenly in the middle of the street

Pirello began to dance. He danced on four legs—one, two, three, hop—one, two, three, hop. The milk cart swayed, and all the bottles rattled and shook. He danced on two legs, with his front legs in the air—one, two, three, hop—one, two, three, hop.

Crates slid from the cart and bottles crashed to the ground. Milk ran in a white river down the street.

"Stop!" cried the milkman, jumping to his feet. "Stop!"

But Pirello didn't stop.

He was a dancing horse. He danced and danced until his act was done. Then he bowed to the cars and bicycles, the people and the children.

Then he stood still.

When the summer market came, Pirello was taken to a far-away village to be sold. He stood silently in the market, as one man after another came to look at him. He didn't care who bought him.

He wanted Carlo and the circus life. His heart was filled with sadness.

Suddenly in the distance he saw
something—something white, flapping in the
wind.   It looked like a tent.   It might be a
circus.   Out of the market ran Pirello, down
the village street, and into the lanes, down
the lanes and into a field.

There he saw tents and caravans.   There he
smelled sawdust and sleeping-boxes.   A
circus!   It was a circus!

Into the big tent ran Pirello.   All the seats

were empty, for it was early in the day, but the band was playing over its music and a clown was trying out his tricks. A girl swung from a trapeze just under the roof.

Ricki, the owner, was in the circus ring watching a man throwing up red and yellow balls and trying to catch them. The man was trying very hard, but he dropped one ball every time.

"It's no good, Carlo," Ricki was saying. "You're not a good juggler. This is the biggest circus in the country, and I want the best people in it. I'm sorry, but you'll have to leave."

Carlo! The juggler was Carlo! Pirello galloped into the ring, and rubbed his head against Carlo's face.

"Pirello" cried Carlo. "Dear Pirello!" Then, hardly daring to believe his eyes, he whispered,

"If you really are Pirello, dance for me."

So Pirello danced. He danced on four legs.

He danced on two legs.   And when the act
was done, he bowed to Ricki and Carlo.

"He's wonderful!" began Ricki, but at that
moment, in came the milkman and a crowd
of people from the market.

"There he is!" cried the milkman,
pointing to Pirello.

"Will you sell him to me?" asked Ricki.

"Certainly," said the milkman.   "I'll be
delighted to do so."

"Carlo," said Ricki, "if I buy this horse,
will you stay with me to be his partner?"

19

"Oh yes," replied Carlo. "You'll find that I'm much better at teaching a horse to dance than I ever shall be at juggling with red and yellow balls."

So at last Pirello the dancing horse danced in a circus for Carlo again. Bright lights. Cheerful music. The soft sawdust of the circus ring. That was the life he loved. It was the only life for a dancing horse.

The Land of White Elephants

Far away in India, when the day's work is done and the night is too hot for sleeping, the children have their story time. This is one of the stories they hear.

Once upon a time there lived a man whose name was Gauba. He looked after the temple gardens, and there he grew flowers and fruit of all kinds.

One night when the moon was full, Gauba
heard the cracking of twigs and the snapping
of stems.   He ran out of his house and saw
a great animal walking in the temple garden.

"Go away!   Go away!" shouted
Gauba, but the animal went on trampling
over the flowers and pushing its way among
the banana plants.   Gauba picked up a stick
to drive it away, but when he came nearer to
it, he stood still in surprise and joy, for the
animal was a white elephant!

There it stood in the moonlight, waving
its long trunk and flapping its large ears.   It
was whiter than the whitest flowers in the
garden.   It was whiter than the whitest
clouds in the summer sky.

It was whiter than the whitest snow on the
mountain tops of India.

A white elephant!   Gauba stared.   He
knew that white elephants hardly ever came
to earth.   He knew that people who saw one
were thought to be very, very lucky.

"Oh elephant," said Gauba, "great white elephant, I *am* lucky to see you."

The white elephant lifted its white trunk, and said,

"I've come from the Land of White Elephants. I've come to give you one wish. What would you like?"

"Oh elephant," replied Gauba, "great white elephant, I should like to go back with you to the Land of White Elephants."

As he spoke, he pulled a large bunch of ripe bananas and gave them to the elephant.

The elephant ate them. Then he said,

"Very well. Next time the moon is full I'll come to the temple garden again. Then you can hold on to my tail, and I'll fly with you to the Land of White Elephants though what you will do there by yourself, I can't think."

"By myself?" replied Gauba. "I'll not be by myself. I'll take my wife and my pet monkey, Kaloo."

The elephant laughed again.   Then

"How can I carry your wife and your pet monkey, Kaloo?" he asked.

"It will be quite easy," said Gauba. "I'll hold your tail.   My wife will cling to my waist; and my pet monkey, Kaloo, will cling round my neck."

The elephant laughed again.   Then suddenly he flew up into the sky, and was soon out of sight.

Gauba gazed up at the clouds and the moonlight, and then down at the flowers and the trees.   Then he hurried indoors to tell his wife the exciting news.   At first she thought he must have been dreaming, but after a while she believed him.

She wasn't pleased at the thought of going to the Land of White Elephants.

"We may not like it there," she said.

"Oh, yes, we shall," replied Gauba.

"We may not get all the things we like to eat."

"Oh, yes, we shall."

"We'll miss our friends and relations."

"Oh, well, we'll have our pet monkey, Kaloo," answered Gauba.   Then he said in a whisper,

"We'll keep it secret.   We won't tell anyone that we're going to the Land of White Elephants."

"Yes," said his wife.   "We'll keep it a secret."

But when Gauba had gone to work in the temple garden the next day, his wife went out—and told the secret to her aunt.

"I should like to come to the Land of White Elephants with you," said her aunt.

"All right," said Gauba's wife.
"Meet me in the temple garden next time there's a full moon, and I'll take you to the Land of White Elephants with us."

Then she told the secret to her uncle.

"I should like to come too," he said.

"Very well," said Gauba's wife.

"Meet me in the temple garden next time
the moon is full, and I'll take you to the
Land of White Elephants too."

Then she told her nephew, and promised
to take him.

Then she told her niece, and promised to
take her.

And when the night of the next full moon
came, Gauba knew that his wife must have
told all her friends and relations, for they
were all in her garden. They were all
waiting to go to the Land of White
Elephants.

Suddenly, down flew the white elephant.
He laughed to see such a crowd of people,
but he thought they had come to wave
goodbye to Gauba, and his wife, and his
pet monkey, Kaloo.

The white elephant knelt down among the
flowers and the banana plants, so that Gauba
could hold his tail.   Kaloo, the pet monkey,
curled himself round Gauba's neck.
Gauba's wife clung round his waist,
and her aunt clung on to her.

Her uncle clung to her aunt.   Her nephew
clung to her uncle.   Her niece clung to her
nephew.   Everyone clung to someone else.

The white elephant waved its white trunk,
flapped its white ears and flew into the sky.
And Gauba and Kaloo, and Gauba's wife,
and all her friends and relations were pulled
up into the sky too.

The white elephant flew over the fields
and the forests.   He flew over the snow-
capped mountains.   He flew on and on

through the clouds and the moonbeams. All
the people holding on made a great noise,
talking and asking each other questions.
But Kaloo, the pet monkey, went to sleep,
curled round Gauba's neck.

"Gauba," said Gauba's wife, "do you
think we'll like living in the Land of White
Elephants?"

"Yes, yes," said Gauba. "I'm sure we
shall."

After a little while, she said,

"Gauba, do you think we'll have to work
as hard in the Land of White Elephants as
we did on the earth?"

"No, no," said Gauba. "We'll not have
to work at all."

After a little while, the wife said,

"Gauba, Auntie wants to know if she will
be able to get fried fish in the Land of
White Elephants."

Before Gauba could answer, the uncle
called out,

"Are there any goats in the Land of White Elephants?"

"I don't know," said Gauba, who wished everyone would be as quiet as his pet monkey, Kaloo.

"Gauba," said his wife again, "do you think there will be water melons in the Land of White Elephants?"

"Of course there will be water melons," said Gauba.

"Oh, good!" said his wife. "How big do you think they'll be?"

"Oh, the usual size," said Gauba rather angrily. "As big as this"—and he spread out his arms, to show how big.

And of course, as he spread out his arms to show her how big, he let go of the white elephant's tail, and fell down to earth again. With him fell his wife, her aunt, her uncle, her nephew, her niece, and all her friends and relations.

Only little Kaloo, the pet monkey, didn't

fall, for he awoke and jumped at once on to the elephant's back, and went flying on to the Land of White Elephants.

Gauba and his wife and all her friends and relations landed safely in the temple garden. They all went back to their homes, and were really quite glad to be back on earth again.

But Gauba was very sad. He didn't mind coming back to earth, but he wanted his pet monkey, Kaloo. Every day he longed and longed for him.

Then one night he heard a tapping at the door. He opened it, and there stood Kaloo.

"Kaloo!" cried Gauba. "How glad I am to see you! Tell me what it was like in the Land of White Elephants."

Kaloo crinkled up his funny little face, and said,

"There were no bananas, no nuts, no water melons."

Then he jumped on to Gauba's shoulder,

curled himself round his neck, and fell asleep.

And that, so the Indians say, is the story of Gauba's journey to the Land of White Elephants.

Adapted

Little Barge Girl

The canal flowed slowly between the flat, green fields. A row of trees leaned over a little, and their moving leaves made dancing patterns on the water.

Down the canal came a barge, pulling

another one behind it. The one in front was loaded with bags of flour, but the one behind was Janine's home, and it was very fine indeed. It had pictures painted round the sides—pictures of castles and roses, and twisting green leaves. It was a beautiful barge.

Father sat at the engine. Mother stood at the back, holding the tiller, which kept the barge going the right way. Janine scrambled about between Mother and

Father; and Janine's cat sat high on the very front as if to say,

"I'm the Canal Cat. This is *my* barge."

Janine was eight years old, and she had lived on the barge all her life. The barge did a six-day journey between two towns, which Janine had always called Flour Town and Wood Town. It took flour down the canal to Wood Town, and wood up the canal to Flour Town.

"Frisky," called Janine to the Canal Cat. "I'll fetch my reading book, and you can do some lessons with me."

She ran down the steps to the cabin below. The cabin had white lace curtains at the window and clean, white covers on the beds. There was a big bed for Mother and Father, and a little one built above it for Janine. There was a mirror fixed upon the wall, and there were cupboards with shiny, brass door knobs.

Janine opened one of the cupboards and

took out a shabby reading book. Then she
ran up into the sunshine again, and sat at
the front of the barge, with Frisky on her
lap.

"You point," she said, "and I'll read."
She held Frisky's paw, and moved it along
the lines as she read the words. She didn't
read as well as most children—but Janine
wasn't able to go to school very often.

She went to school in Wood Town for two
or three days while Father was unloading the
flour and putting on the wood.

Then when the barge left Wood Town, there was no more school till she came back in another two weeks.

"Now you read, Frisky," she said, and Frisky purred almost as loudly as the barge engine. He was a young cat, not much more than a kitten, and he let Janine play all sorts of games with him.

"You're a lovely cat," Janine would say. "You're as good as a brother or sister would be." And so he was!

Then Mother said to Janine,

"You take the tiller a little while, so that I can peel potatoes for dinner." So Mother went below to find the potatoes, and Janine kept the barge going the right way. She felt very proud of herself as she sailed down the calm canal, between the flat, green fields and the tall trees.

Almost as soon as Mother had gone, Janine saw another barge coming in the distance. She watched as it came nearer.

Then she called,

"Father, Father, it's Henry's barge.
Please may I stop and play with him?"

Father called to Mother,

"Barge in sight!"

Mother came up to take the tiller, without
stopping to finish the potatoes. Janine ran
back to the front, and stood up to watch the
barge come nearer. Oh, how pleased she
was, for Henry was her best friend.
Henry's barge had pictures painted round
the sides too—pictures of castles and roses
and twisting green leaves, but it was not
quite as beautiful as Janine's.

Henry's father carried coal on his barge.
Sometimes he was late, and sometimes
Janine's father was late, and so there was no
time to stop and talk. Then the two fathers
would shout their news as they passed, and
the two children would wave and call,

"Hello! Goodbye!"

But today there was time—a whole hour

to play with Henry.   Mother steered the
barge close to the bank; and Henry's mother
steered his barge close to Janine's.   A line of
washing waved above Henry's deck, and a
little trail of coal dust floated on the water.

In a moment the children were on the
grassy bank, playing "catch" across the
fields.   In a moment the mothers and fathers
were talking to one another, and Frisky the
Canal Cat was chasing a bird up a tree.

But oh, the hour went so quickly.   Janine
told Henry a new game she had made up,

for playing alone.   Henry showed Janine
some new sums he had learned at school.
They climbed a tree and swung on a low
branch.   They played ball.   They laughed
and chatted—and then the hour was gone!

"Janine!" called Mother.   "It's time we
went."

"Come along, Henry," called Henry's
mother. "We're just going."

Janine's father went to the engine. Her
mother went to the tiller, and steered the
barge away from the bank and down the
canal again. Janine waved to Henry and
watched his barge go on its way. She
watched the line of washing waving in the
breeze, and the little trail of coal dust in the
water.

Then Mother called,

"Janine, I'll cook the potatoes now, if you'll take the tiller."

★　★　★　★　★　★

After dinner, Janine found paper and pencil and showed Mother the sums that Henry had taught her. She did a great many of them, and Mother marked them for her. She was so busy that it was nearly tea time before she thought of Frisky the Canal Cat.

"Frisky," she called, "come and play with me." But Frisky didn't come.

"Frisky!" called Janine. "Frisky!" She looked all round the barge, from end to end. She went below and looked in the cabin. She looked under the beds. She even looked inside the cupboards with the shiny, brass door knobs, but she couldn't find Frisky anywhere.

"Don't worry," said Mother. "I expect he's asleep among the flour sacks. Will you fill the kettle for tea, and tell me when it boils?"

Janine went to the cabin again, and poured water from the water jug into the kettle. There were two water jugs, and they both had pictures painted on them. The pictures were of castles and roses and twisting leaves, like the ones round the barge. Janine lit the small oil stove and put the kettle on to boil.

Soon tea was ready and over, and evening passed. It began to grow dark, and Father tied the barges up for the night.

"Bedtime, Janine," said Mother.

"Oh, please let me fetch Frisky from the flour sacks," said Janine. She climbed into the front barge and looked among the flour sacks, but Frisky the Canal Cat wasn't there.

"Oh, Mother," cried Janine, growing suddenly worried, "Frisky is lost. We must have left him behind when we stopped this morning."

Mother and Father looked everywhere, but they couldn't find Frisky.

"I saw him run up a tree," wailed Janine. "He must still be there. Or perhaps he fell in the water and was drowned. Oh, Father, we'll have to go back and look for him."

"We can't do that," said Father. "It would take a whole day to get there and back—and I can't be late with the flour."

"Oh, please let's go back," begged Janine, beginning to cry.

"You go to bed," said Father kindly. "I expect Frisky is somewhere around.

We're sure to find him.   Mother and I will have another look when you're in bed."

Sadly Janine undressed, and climbed into the wooden bunk above the big bed where Mother and Father slept.   Frisky the Canal Cat was lost.   He might be drowned in the water.   He might be running along the bank, looking for the barge.   He might still be up in the tree, where she had seen him last.

Sadly Janine listened to the water lapping against the side of the barge.   She listened for a long while—a long while, until she fell asleep.

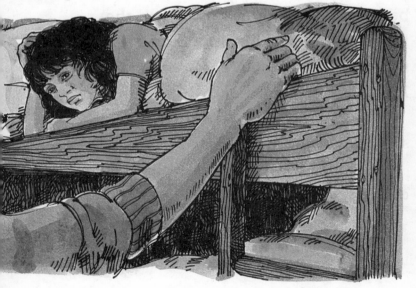

Janine was most unhappy. Frisky the Canal Cat was really lost, and she was so lonely without him.

"Never mind," said Mother and Father. "We'll buy you another cat soon."

"I don't want another cat," said Janine. "I want Frisky."

Even two days' school at Wood Town didn't cheer her up very much. But she felt a little better when Father promised to stop on the way back, and ask people in houses near the bank if they had found Frisky the Canal Cat.

So the barge started sailing up the canal, between the flat, green fields and the swaying trees. This time the barge in front was filled with wood, going on its way to Flour Town.

After three days' journey back, Mother said, as usual,

"Hold the tiller, Janine, while I see to the dinner."

Janine took the tiller, while Mother went below to wash some carrots. Janine stood sadly, staring at the water and thinking of Frisky, when suddenly she saw another barge coming in the distance. She waited a few moments as it came nearer. Then she called,

"Father, Father! It's Henry's barge. Please may I stop and play with him?"

"Not this time, I'm afraid," said Father. Then he called to Mother,

"Barge in sight."

Mother came running up to take the tiller, without stopping to finish the carrots. Janine stood at the front of the barge, waiting to shout, "Hello! Goodbye!" to Henry.

Henry's barge came nearer, with its pictures of castles and roses and twisting leaves. There was his mother at the tiller and his father at the engine. There was the line of clean washing, and the little trail of coal dust.

"Where's Henry?" murmured Janine. "Oh, there he is. Hello Henry!"

But Henry was shouting out in excitement, and holding something up for Janine to see. Janine's heart gave a little jump of joy, for Henry was holding up Frisky the Canal Cat!

So the barge had to stop for a few minutes after all, while Henry put Frisky into Janine's eager arms.

As for Frisky the Canal Cat, he jumped to his old place at the very front of Janine's barge, and there he sat, purring as if to say,

"I'm the Canal Cat. *This* is my barge."

A Mother for a Lion

There was once a little lion cub whose
mother had been killed by hunters.   He
wasn't nearly old enough to look after
himself, but there he was all alone in the
African bush.

At first the little lion cub was frightened, so he ran and ran until he saw the blue sea sparkling in the distance. Then he was tired, so he opened his mouth in a wide yawn, and he blinked his yellow eyes. He curled himself up in a patch of dust, and he fell asleep.

And there—two sailors found him. A cargo ship was in port near by, and the sailors had come to spend an hour or two on the beach.

"Look!" said one in surprise. "A lion cub!"

"Be careful," whispered the other. "His mother may come out in a minute."

They waited, but nothing moved in the bushes and the lion cub went on sleeping.

"He looks too small to be left alone," said the first sailor. He bent down and lifted up the little lion cub. The lion cub opened his yellow eyes and crinkled up his nose. He stretched his front legs and patted the sailor's face with soft little paws. The sailors laughed.

They sat on the ground and began to play with the lion cub, as they might have played with a kitten. They rolled him on his back and stroked his furry chest. They put their hands in his mouth, and let him pretend to bite them. They laughed and talked, and played with him for a long while.

"It's time we went back to the ship," said one at last.   He stood the little lion cub on its feet, and said,

"Goodbye, little one.   Run along home now."

But when the sailors started to walk away, the lion cub followed them, ran over their feet and bit their shoe laces.

"No, no," said the sailors.   They pushed him gently into the bushes, and they hurried back along the dusty road to the port, but the lion cub ran out again.   He tumbled over their feet, dug his claws into their socks and tried to bite their shoes.   He would *not* let the sailors go.

The sailors stood still and looked at each other.

"Let's take him back to the ship," said the first.

"It seems strange for a lion cub to be walking about alone," said the second. "I wonder where his mother is."

"She may have been killed by a hunter," said the first.

Just then the lion cub clawed at the sailor's leg and growled, as if to say,

"Yes, yes. That's what happened. Please take me with you."

The second sailor picked the lion cub up again, and said,

"Oh, all right—but you'll have to keep those sharp claws hidden."

The lion cub crinkled up his nose, and blinked his yellow eyes. Then he opened his mouth in a wide yawn and fell asleep in the sailor's arms.

Next time he awoke, he found himself on a cargo ship, sailing out across the sea.

He gave one long look at the shores of Africa lying like a thin, white cloud between the blue sky and the blue sea. Then he stretched and yawned, and started to explore his new home.

He smelled all sorts of new smells. He

sniffed at everything he found.   He peeped
into cabins and cupboards.   He climbed on
to beds and bunks.   He played with dozens
of sailors, and then he found a dog.

Jess, the ship's dog, was lying on deck,
with her nose on her front paws.   She was
sad because her puppies had been taken from
her and sold a few days before.

She was so sad, she didn't even see the
little lion cub in front of her.

The little lion cub stretched one paw and
patted Jess on the nose.   Jess sat up and
growled softly.   She wasn't at all sure what
sort of animal this was.

The little lion cub wasn't afraid.   He slid
his front legs along the deck, and stuck his
tail up in the air, like a puppy wanting to
play.   Jess wagged her tail.   This funny
little animal was something like one of her
own puppies.   He was small and fluffy and
playful, and he needed someone to look after
him.

She stood up and sniffed at him. Then
suddenly she rolled him over on his back,
and began to play with him.

The sailors who were near, called others to
come and look. They laughed aloud, as Jess
and the lion cub chased each other across the
deck, and rolled over together, pretending to
bite and growl.

Then at last, when Jess was panting, and
the little lion cub was tired, the two animals
cuddled up together, and fell asleep. And
so the friendship started between the little
lion cub and Jess, the ship's dog.

For many months the ship sailed the seas. The lion cub was playful and friendly, and all the sailors loved him. Jess was like a mother to him, and the two animals spent nearly all their time together.

But the lion cub grew very quickly, and the sailors found it hard to feed him. They were still fond of him, but they didn't play with him so often now, because his teeth and claws were getting too sharp.

"What shall we do with him?" they sometimes said. "He's bigger than Jess now. He'll soon grow even more, and we can hardly keep a full-grown lion walking about on deck."

"We'd better give him to a zoo when we reach home," said one sailor. "Then we can visit him."

So when the ship reached home, the sailors gave the lion cub to a zoo.

"We'll come and see you tomorrow," they said, for the ship was to be in port for five days. They said goodbye, and waved their hands. The lion cub blinked his yellow eyes and opened his mouth in a wide yawn, for he did not really understand.

But that night, as he lay in a strange, dark cage, he felt lonely and unhappy. He missed the sailors, and most of all he missed Jess, his dog mother. He walked up and down in the cage, and pressed himself against the bars. He stared at the stars twinkling in the sky.

Then he opened his mouth as widely as he could, and he roared and roared.

Next morning, almost as soon as the zoo opened, in came the sailors, leading Jess on a piece of rope. They went up to the lion cub's cage, saying,

"Hello, little one. How do you feel today?"

As they spoke, Jess gave a yelp of joy and jerked her rope free; and in one second, she had slipped through the bars to her friend.

Oh, how pleased the lion cub was to see her! He sniffed at her in delight and patted her gently with his paw. Then the two animals sat down together in the straw, and both of them were happy again.

It was useless for the sailors to call and whistle to Jess. She kept just out of reach. She lifted her head, and wagged her tail, but she wouldn't leave the lion cub. None of the zoo keepers liked the idea of going into the cage to take her out—so there she stayed.

Next week the ship sailed—without the lion cub, and without Jess.

The lion cub grew into a fine, big lion, so that Jess looked quite small beside him. And the story says (for it is a true one) that Jess and the lion lived happily together for the rest of their lives.

People came from all over the country to see them, and were amazed at their strange friendship.

The First Lamp

Lok and Shan sat by the fire in their new
cave.   It was large and warm and dry.
Baby crawled across the floor, playing some
game of his own.   Small Baby, who was
very young, was wrapped up in a bearskin
and was fast asleep in a corner.   Mother and
Father had gone out in the tree-trunk boat.

The sun was sinking low in the sky.   But
though it was still quite light in the open air,
the cave was almost in darkness, except just
now and then when the fire gave a little
glow.

Small Baby awoke and began to cry.

Shan went over to the corner of the cave where he was lying. It was so dark there that she couldn't see Small Baby at all, but when she put out her hand to him, she could feel that he had lost his bearskin.

"You're cold," she said, and she moved about on her hands and knees, feeling for the bearskin. Then she wrapped Small Baby up tightly and sang him to sleep.

"Mother and Father are a long time," said Lok, when Shan came back to sit by the fire.

"Yes," replied Shan. Then she said, "This cave is very dark."

"All caves are dark," answered Lok.

The children sat talking and laughing in the firelight. They watched the patch of daylight in the doorway grow more and more dim. Baby crawled near the fire. He curled up beside Lok and fell asleep.

The fire crackled and glowed. The patch of light in the doorway grew more and more dim.

Lok became sleepy, and had just closed his eyes when he heard a tiny rustle of leaves outside.

"Mother and Father coming home," he thought, and he looked up at the doorway.

Oh! His heart stood still with fear. There in the entrance of the cave was a tiger—wild and hungry, cruel and fierce.

For a second, Shan noticed nothing wrong and went on talking,

"We'd better put Baby to bed," she said. Then she saw the look of terror on Lok's face. She looked up to see what had frightened him, and she too saw the tiger in the doorway—wild and hungry, fierce and cruel.

Shan screamed at the top of her voice! She grabbed a bit of burning branch from the fire and rushed towards the doorway. She waved the burning branch right in the tiger's face. The sudden dazzling brightness startled him. He gave a low growl of fear and slunk away into the forest.

Baby awoke and began to cry loudly.
Small Baby awoke and started crying too.
Lok ran to the doorway and looked both
ways to make sure that the tiger had gone.
Then he stood in the cave and laughed.

"Clever Shan!" said he. "She frightened
the tiger away with a little bit of fire on a
stick."

But Shan leaned against the wall of the
cave, still holding the burning branch, and
still trembling with fright.

"Clever Shan!" shouted Lok again. "She
frightened the tiger away with a little bit of
fire on a stick."

Baby cried more loudly than before, and Small Baby simply screamed.

"Oh, do be quiet everyone," said Shan. "Lok, make Baby stop crying." She walked to the far corner of the cave to comfort Small Baby, still holding the lighted branch. She leaned over Small Baby. His face was red and unhappy. She could see him quite clearly.

"This is good," she thought to herself. "The burning branch makes a light for the cave."

There was a wide crack in the rocky wall just above her head. She reached up and fixed the end of the branch in it. The top flared and went on burning. It gave a most beautiful patch of light.

"Now I can see you," said Shan to Small Baby. She tucked him up and talked to him, and he stopped crying and fell asleep again.

"Lok," said Shan, "I've made a light for the cave."

But Lok was playing with Baby by the
fire, and making him laugh at the story of
how Shan frightened the tiger away with a
little bit of fire on a stick.

"Lok!" said Shan again.   "I've made a
light for the cave."

This time Lok looked.

"What a good idea!" he said. "Let's make another."

"I know where there's another crack in the wall," said Shan. "Just above the shelf of rock where the food and the tools of flint are kept."

Lok pulled a broken branch from the fire, but it was no good because it was burning all the way along. So he found one that was burning only at the end, and he fixed it in the crack above the shelf of rock where the food and the tools of flint were kept.

Now there were two burning branches fixed high in the walls, blazing brightly and making the cave quite light.

"Now we can see even at night," said Shan. Lok jumped and danced in excitement, and sang a new song,

"We've made light for the dark, dark cave!" Shan and Baby joined in, and they all made so much noise that they didn't even hear Mother and Father come in.

Mother and Father stood inside the
doorway and looked round in surprise.

"How light it is in here," said Father.
"Yet it's almost dark outside."

"How nice the cave looks," said Mother.
"It's as light as day."

"We've made lights," replied Lok and
Shan. "Come and look."

Baby climbed up into Mother's arms and twisted his fat little fingers in her long, tangled hair. Then Mother and Father went to look at the lights that the children had made.

"They're wonderful," said Mother. "We'll always do that when we want light now."

"It's a good idea," said Father. Then they all sat round the fire. Mother and Father listened in wonder to the story of how Shan

frightened the tiger away with a little bit of
fire on the end of a stick.

And as they talked and laughed, light
shone in the dark corner where Small Baby
slept, and light shone above the shelf of rock
where the food and the tools of flint were
kept.

Baby grew tired, and fell asleep on
Mother's lap, but Mother, Father, Lok and
Shan talked for a long while in the light of
the first lamps in the world.

The Tapestry

Ali stood at the open door of the workroom, and looked longingly inside.   His sister was there with a number of other children.
Most of them were about ten years old.   Ali watched them.

Some were sitting on the floor, sorting out heaps of wool and choosing the colours they wanted.   There were all sorts of colours.
There were reds and blues and yellows.
There were greys and browns and greens.
There was black.   There was white.   There was purple.   Ali longed to choose some for himself.

Some of the children were sitting on benches, with upright, wooden looms in front of them.   They were weaving.   They were pushing the wool in and out of the strings, and making pictures and patterns.
This was what Ali wanted to do most of all.

The owner of the workroom was called Mr Ramses. He saw Ali standing at the door, and he walked over to him.

"Hello," he said.

"Please," said Ali with a sudden burst of courage, "please may I come and weave pictures too ?"

"I'm afraid not," replied Mr Ramses. "I can't take any more children. There isn't room."

He was sorry to disappoint this little boy.
"How old are you?" he asked kindly.

"Eight," said Ali.

"Perhaps when you're older there might
be a space for you."

Mr Ramses went back into the room, and
Ali wandered away. He went home because
it was very hot out in the sun. He sat on
the floor and wished and wished that he
could join his sister and weave pictures in
the afternoons.

It was really his own fault that he wasn't
working. When Mr Ramses had first come
to the village and asked who would like to
join his workroom, Ali hadn't gone.

Mr Ramses had been an art teacher in
Cairo. Then he had bought a piece of land
in Ali's village, near the Great Pyramids, and
he had opened the workroom. It was just
for children. He had taken any child who
had wanted to come, and he had explained
to them what he was trying to do.

"In past days," he had said, "the people
of Egypt did beautiful paintings. They
made beautiful pots of clay and statues of
stone. They spun wool from their sheep
and goats, and they wove beautiful pictures.
They were called tapestries.

"But nowadays, hardly anyone makes
beautiful things. People buy them from
shops and factories. They have forgotten
how to paint and weave and make pots.
Soon these skills and arts will be lost to
Egypt for ever, but you, the children, can
help to save them. I believe that every
child can be an artist and make beautiful
things."

So now, there they were, the children of
Ali's village, weaving nearly every
afternoon. Mr Ramses showed them how to
push the wool in and out of the strings.

"Tell me a story in wool," he would say,
and soon he was surprised at the pictures
that grew on the looms. Then as the weeks
went by, he was simply amazed! The
children wove scenes showing camels and
sheep, palm trees and houses. They knew
just how to use the colours. They began to
make really beautiful tapestries.

"Every child can be an artist," Mr Ramses had said. This was something he had always believed. Now he was seeing it come true.

But Ali was an artist too. He knew he had pictures inside himself. He knew he would be able to weave them on a loom if only he had the chance.

He started going to the workroom every afternoon, and watching the other children. Mr Ramses didn't seem to mind. Ali was very quiet. He watched the children push their little balls of wool between the strings. He watched them weave their patterns and pictures. He watched them snip off the tiny, short ends of wool that were left over.

"Please," Ali would say softly, "may I have the bits you are going to throw away?"

He collected a handful. He did it every day. Mr Ramses didn't mind. He knew Ali would take the soft, coloured scraps of wool home and play with them.

But Ali did more than that. He found some bits of wood and some string, and he made himself a simple little loom. Then with great, great patience, he tied the tiny, short scraps of wool together, and he began to poke them in and out of the strings. Slowly, slowly he began to weave a pattern in different colours. He was happy. He was weaving his own tapestry.

A few days later, when the pattern was finished, he took it to the workroom, half hiding it, but wanting it to be seen.

"Hello, Ali," said Mr Ramses. "What have you got there?"

"A tapestry," whispered Ali. "I made it."

"You made it?" said Mr Ramses. "And you made your own small loom?"

"Yes," nodded Ali.

Mr Ramses smiled. How *could* he turn away this eight-year-old boy who had shown such patience, and who so badly wanted to join the workroom?

"Ali," he said, "you may start coming next week. We'll *make* room for you."

So, to his great delight, Ali joined the other children and did everything that they did.

Mr Ramses taught them how to spin wool from the clippings of sheep and goats. He taught them how to colour the wool with dyes made from plants. He told them which plant, or mixture of plants, would make a blue dye, which would make a green one and which would make a yellow one.

Sometimes he gave them new ideas for their weaving, by taking them for walks. He took them into the desert, or beside the River Nile. He even took them to the zoo, in Cairo.

Then one day, he took the best of the tapestries and put them on show in Cairo. Many people came to see them, and they were amazed that children could do such good work.

Some of the young weavers

at work in Mr Ramses' workroom.

Some people bought the woven pictures.
"They are just as beautiful as the
tapestries of old," they said.

So the work grew and grew. Mr Ramses
paid the children for their pictures, and he
bought more land so that they could grow
their own plants for making dyes. He also
built a better workroom and held shows in

other cities, not only in Egypt, but in many countries in Europe too.

Some of the children's woven pictures are now in museums in different countries; and there are many places in Egypt where the old arts and crafts are starting again.

As for Ali, he is grown up now, and he is one of the best of Egypt's weavers.

The Boy who Loved Animals

Edwin loved animals.   Even when he was a baby, he used to hold out his arms to passing horses, or stroke the smooth coat of his father's dog.   His father was an artist and his big brothers were going to be artists too.

So while he was still very small, they gave him pencil and paper, and they watched eagerly to see if his scribbles were better than the scribbles of other babies.

"I think he *will* be an artist," said his father.

"I wonder what he'll draw," said his mother.

And Edwin of course, as he grew older, drew animals, for he loved animals and animals loved him.

In those days there were farms and fields in London, and Edwin would climb on

fences and stare at cows and pigs; or he
would walk to the zoo, which was then at
the Tower of London.

When he was five years old, his father took him for a walk in the country. They came to a field, where a cow lay resting. Edwin's father lifted him over the gate and said,

"See if you can draw that cow."

Edwin drew it. Carefully he drew the shape of its body and head. He noticed its big eyes and the tufts of fur inside its ears. He noticed the markings on its smooth coat and the way its legs rested on the grass.

All these things he put down on the paper. Then, when he had finished, he held the paper up to his father and said,

"There you are."

"It's very good indeed," said his father.
"But you haven't made the legs quite right."

He bent down beside Edwin and showed
him how to make the drawing better. Then
they went home to tea.

That night, his father put the picture away
in a safe place, for he was very proud of it.
It was a better picture of a cow than lots of
grown-up people could have drawn; and for
a little boy of five, it was wonderful.

Often after that, Edwin went with his
brothers to a field near by. They sat on the
grass and took out their sketch books. They
drew pigs, sheep, donkeys, or whatever they
saw.

When it was tea time, their father came to
fetch them, but before he took them home to
tea, he looked at their pictures and showed
them how to change them here and there, to
make them look better.

So as Edwin grew older, he filled papers
and drawing books with pictures of
animals—farm animals in the fields, lions
and tigers in the zoo, and of course dogs, all
sorts of dogs.

Dogs seemed to know that Edwin was
their friend.   Stray dogs always seemed to
come to him.   Even fierce watchdogs rubbed
themselves against his legs and waited for
him to stroke them.

One day when Edwin was in the town by himself, he saw a huge dog. It was a Saint Bernard, the largest dog he had ever seen.

"Oh!" thought Edwin. "If only he would stand still and let me draw him!"

But the dog took such long strides, and walked so quickly that Edwin had to run to keep up with him.

"Oh, I *must* draw him," thought Edwin, "perhaps he'll stand still soon."

Along the street went the great Saint Bernard, round the corner, across a square, down another street. After him went Edwin, hurrying to keep up.

Soon the dog turned in at a gate and disappeared round the back of a house. Edwin walked up the path and knocked at the door.

"Please," he said to the man who answered, "may I draw a picture of your dog?" The man was surprised, but he said, "Yes. Come inside."

He took Edwin to a room where the Saint Bernard dog had stretched himself out on the floor to rest. Edwin sat on a chair, took paper and pencil from his pocket and began to draw.

So the years went on, and Edwin drew big and small dogs, sad and happy dogs; and by the time he was grown up, everyone in London had heard of Edwin Landseer, the artist who drew dogs.

One day Queen Victoria sent for him and asked him to draw pictures of all her pets. This made Edwin very happy, for there were all kinds of dogs in the palace—black ones and brown ones, curly ones and smooth ones. Sometimes the Queen came to watch him at his work.

"How do you make your dogs look so real?" she asked one day.

"Your Majesty," said Edwin, "I peep into their hearts."

Some of Queen Victoria's pets. (*Right*) One of her favourite dogs, a King Charles' spaniel called Dash. (*Opposite*) A macaw, two love birds, a Skye terrier called Islay and a toy spaniel called Tilco.

"Can you draw children too?" asked the Queen.

"Yes, I can," replied Edwin.

"Then will you paint pictures of my children for me?"

So when the palace dogs were finished, Edwin Landseer painted pictures of the little princes and princesses, but he nearly always put a dog in the pictures too.

So he became famous, and hundreds of people wanted to buy his pictures. He painted and painted and painted. He painted dogs and lions and deer, and always as he painted, a real dog would sit at his feet.

★ ★ ★ ★ ★ ★

If you want to see something of Edwin Landseer's work, go to Trafalgar Square in London. There, fountains splash and pigeons fly; and in the middle of the square are four great lions made of bronze.

Proudly they sit, looking at London and watching the people passing by.

They have been there a long while now and many things have happened since first they came. Perhaps they don't remember much, or anything at all. But perhaps they remember the man who made them and the dog who always lay at his feet.

For the great lions of bronze in Trafalgar Square were made by Edwin Landseer, the boy who loved animals.

Anansi the Spider

Have you heard of Anansi?

Long ago, people in Jamaica told stories about Anansi and his friends, and these tales have been passed down from one family to another.

Anansi is really a spider. But sometimes he changes into a human being. He talks and behaves like a human.

He is very clever and is always playing tricks. Anansi is a thief. He won't work for his living if he can steal or cheat to get food or money.

But somehow people still laugh at him— even when he is up to his tricks. Maybe it's because he is cheerful. He is always in a good temper, even when he is doing something wicked.

There are lots of other animals in the Anansi stories—Tiger and Crab and Monkey and Hare and Tortoise. They, too, talk and behave like human beings.

You will find Anansi stories in West Africa too. But Anansi himself is always the same—half spider, half human. And he is always playing tricks both on humans and animals.

Here are some stories about Anansi.

How Anansi saved Monkey

Anansi and his good friend Monkey were travelling together when all of a sudden they saw Tiger in a hole.

"Look!" cried Anansi. "We must help poor Brother Tiger. But what can I do? I'm only a spider. You can help, Monkey. Why don't you climb down into the hole and help Tiger out?"

"All right," said Monkey. "I will."

But where was Anansi? He was already up a tree, watching from a safe place.

Monkey put his long tail into the hole and
Tiger climbed up the tail.

But as soon as Tiger was on the ground,
he seized Monkey.

"I've got you! I've got you!" he cried out
in triumph.

Anansi looked down from the tree.
"Brother Tiger, now that you've got
Monkey, are you going to eat him?"

"Yes," said Tiger with a roar, "I am."

"You must be very pleased," said
Anansi.   "Why don't you open your paws
and clap for joy and say, 'I've got
Monkey!'"

"Yes, yes," said Tiger.   He opened his
paws and clapped them together for joy.
"I've got Monkey!" he cried out.

And so Monkey escaped, and he ran away
as fast as he could.

* * * * * * *

Sometimes Anansi does help people—but it
is always for a reward.

The Man who Couldn't Talk

Once there was a poor man who couldn't talk.   The king of the country wanted to help him.   If only he could make the dumb man speak!

At last he had an idea.

"I'll give one of my three daughters," he said, "to anyone who can make this dumb man talk."

Anansi heard of this. He went to the hog and asked him, "If I take you to the dumb man, what will you say?"

"Ugh! Ugh!" said the hog.

"No," said Anansi. "That won't do."

Then Anansi went to the goat. The goat was nibbling grass.

"If I take you to the dumb man," he said, "what will you say?"

"Me-eh," said the goat.

"No," said Anansi. "That won't do."

Then he went to the chicken.

"If I take you to the dumb man," he said, "what will you say?"

"Cluck! Cluck!" said the chicken.

"Oh, no," said Anansi. "That won't do at all."

Last of all he went to the peafowl. The peafowl sang most beautifully to him.

"Will you come with me and sing to the dumb man?" asked Anansi.

"Yes," said the peafowl. "I will."

So Anansi and the peafowl went to the palace.

"We're here to see the dumb man," said Anansi. "My friend the peafowl will sing."

So Anansi and the peafowl went before the king and the dumb man, and the peafowl began to sing.

At first, the dumb man simply listened. And then, as he listened to the song of the peafowl, he began to hum very quietly.

The peafowl sang even more sweetly. And the dumb man began to hum louder and louder. Then at last, he burst into song, singing the words of the peafowl's song himself.

"This is amazing!" cried the king.

The dumb man sang and sang and went on to speak of the beautiful music of the peafowl.

The king said, "Anansi, you deserve the reward. You will marry one of my daughters."

Anansi was very pleased. He was so pleased that he gave the peafowl a reward too. He gave him gold to put all over his body and plenty of corn to eat.

And that is why, to this day, the peafowl is covered in gold.

★　★　★　★　★　★

In the next story, Anansi is back to his tricks again.

Anansi and Mosquito

An old woman had a daughter, but no one knew the girl's name. The old woman said, "I will give one hundred pounds to anyone who can find out my daughter's name."

Anansi heard this. He said, "I must win this reward of a hundred pounds." He thought and thought. Then he went to Mosquito.

"Let's find out the girl's name," said Anansi. "You go into her room, because you're very small and can go through cracks in the floor. I'll go into the mother's room below."

"Very well," Mosquito agreed.

In the middle of the night, when all was dark and quiet, Mosquito crept into the girl's room.

He sang into her ear.

The girl, in her sleep, brushed at her ear and said, "Go away!"

Down below, Anansi was hidden in the
mother's room, listening.

Mosquito went back a second time to the
girl's room and sang into her ear.

"Go away!" said the girl, brushing her
ear.   And still Anansi listened.   A third
time, Mosquito went to the girl's bedside,
and sang into her ear.

"Go away!" cried the girl in her sleep.
"Go away!"

Down below, the mother heard. She
called out to her daughter, "Zegrady!
Zegrady! What's wrong?"

The girl woke up. "Nothing, Mother.
Just something that worried me in my
sleep."

And she went back to sleep again.

Anansi had heard the mother call. He ran
off as fast as he could. When he reached
home, he took up his fiddle and sang a little
song,

"Zegrady, Zegrady, Zegra, Zegrady . . .
Come shake Anansi's hand, my dear."

Next morning he went to the old woman's house and played his fiddle and sang his song outside.

"Come in, come in," said the old woman, and she gave Anansi the reward of a hundred pounds.

How pleased Anansi was!

But he didn't give anything to Mosquito. Nothing at all!

How angry Mosquito was!

He's still angry to this day. That's why Mosquito still flies at people, making an angry noise and stinging them. He hasn't forgotten how Anansi cheated him.

Adapted by Anne Forsyth

A Horse for a Prince

Clatter, clatter, clatter!   It was the sound of
a horse's hooves in the palace yard.
Alexander the Prince went to the window,
and looked down below.

Oh, what a horse!   Alexander's father was
a king, and the palace stables were the finest
in the country, but even so, the young
prince had never seen a horse as beautiful
as this.

Its glossy, jet-black coat shone in the
bright sunlight.   Its head tossed proudly,
and its eyes had the gleam of fire in them.
It was so full of life and spirit, that the man
who led it could scarcely hold the reins.

Oh, what a horse!   As soon as he saw it,
Alexander wanted it for his own.

"Hello!" he called.   "Whose horse?"
The man looked up, and saw him.

"Whose horse?" shouted Alexander again.

"It's mine," replied the man, "but I hope to sell it to the king."

Down the steps went Alexander, and out into the palace yard. By that time the king was there, with a number of servants, and men from the stables.

"Who will try this horse?" asked the king.

"I will," cried the head stable-man. He walked over to the horse, but before he could get near, the horse tossed its head wildly and kicked out with its legs.

Patiently the head stable-man waited till it was calmer. Then he went up to it again, but it was no good. The horse was so fearful and frisky, that the man couldn't get anywhere near it.

"Let someone else try," said the king.

"I will!" cried the second stable-man. He moved silently up to the horse from the back, and managed to catch hold of the rein. In a second, the horse was plunging and kicking, stamping angrily with its hooves, and tossing its head wildly. The second stable-man lost the rein at once and fell heavily to the ground.

"It's a beautiful horse," said the king. "But it's no use to me unless it can be ridden. Is there no one here who can ride it?"

One after another, horsemen and stable-men tried. But the horse stood up on its back legs, or plunged forward, kicking in all directions. Its jet-black coat shone in the bright sunlight. Its head tossed wildly and its eyes had the gleam of fire in them. One or two men managed to hold on to the reins for a minute, but no one could calm the horse and stay on its back.

"Oh, what a horse!" thought Alexander.
"If only I could have it for my own!"

"It's a beautiful horse," said the king
again, "but I'm afraid it's no use to me."

"Oh, dear!" exclaimed Alexander.
"We're losing this fine horse just because
our men are not brave enough or clever
enough to manage it."

"Hush," said the king.   "That's not the
way to speak about our men.   They're older
and wiser than you."

"But still they don't know how to manage
this fine horse."

"Well," replied the king, a little angrily, "could you do it?"

"Oh, yes," cried Alexander.

"All right," said the king. "You may try. If you can ride the horse, you may have it for yourself."

The people in the palace yard leaned forward eagerly to see if anyone else would try. When they saw the young Prince Alexander walk bravely forward, they laughed aloud.

But Alexander noticed something. He noticed that as the horse kicked and pranced, its shadow kicked and pranced on the ground before it. The horse was frightened by its own shadow. So Alexander caught hold of the reins and managed to turn the horse, so that its shadow fell behind it.

Then he stroked its glossy coat and spoke gently to it. The horse kicked and plunged and tossed its head. The king's heart was filled with terror and he wished he hadn't allowed the prince to go. The horse was wild, and no one could tame it. Alexander would be killed!

The king opened his lips to call the prince back. Then he closed them without speaking, for Alexander had managed somehow to keep hold of the reins. He was still talking gently to the horse—and it almost seemed as if the horse was beginning to trust him. Suddenly Alexander slipped on to its back.

There was one terrible moment when the horse tried to throw him to the ground. The people gasped in horror. The king was silent with fear for his son, but Alexander clung on, and the horse couldn't shake itself free of him.

After a little while the horse became